Three Dates

TROUBLED GIRLS FIND LOVE

KATHRYN REIGN

KATHRYN REIGN PUBLISHING

Copyright

Three Dates

© Copyright 2023 Kathryn Reign

Any references to historical events, real people, or real places are used fictitiously. Names, characters, and places are products of the author's imagination.

Cover Design by Les (germancreative)

Three Dates

Three Dates Blurb

Amelia Ainsworth wasn't looking for an arranged marriage, but she had finally given in to her aunt's pleas to set her up on a date with what Evelyne called "the perfect match." All she knows about Alistair is that he's the son of her friend, Merlyn, and a smart, kind-hearted young man in medical school.

And it certainly doesn't hurt that he's both handsome and charming.

He's her date for three nights. That's the deal. Three dates set up by her aunt as her dying wish. The first one goes smoothly. But it's like being on a set, playing a part. Doing what's expected of them.

However, by date number three, she finds herself running away from him and into the arms of another man.

And now Amelia is starting to regret having made that decision.

Is it too late to turn back?

Can she apologize for her mistake and get Alistair to forgive her?

Or did she just push away the potential love of her life forever?

Contents

Chapter One

"Ow! What the fuck?" Amelia Ainsworth hissed loudly as she sprung her head up from in between her arms. She looked over at her best friend, Melody Kim, who was glaring at her as if something bad were going to happen soon... very, very soon.

"I see you're using my class as your own personal naptime again, Ms. Ainsworth."

Amelia looked up, just to find the entire lecture hall of eighty plus students staring at her, some smirking, many chuckling. Her physics professor, Professor Ambone, stood at the front with his arms crossed over his chest.

"S-Sorry," she apologized half-heartedly. "I was up late last night."

"That's...," Ambone paused to count his fingers, "the thirteenth time this month. Either you need a doctor to cure that problematic narcolepsy of yours, or I suggest you pull yourself together to avoid failing my class."

More chuckles echoed throughout the lecture hall, and Amelia clenched her fists together, her nails digging deep into her skin.

"Y-Yes, sir," she mumbled.

"I sure hope so, Ms. Ainsworth. And oh, you might want to clean up your face a bit. You got some dribble beginning to crust on the side of your mouth." He then turned to the rest of the class. "Class dismissed. And don't forget the final exam the week after spring break. I'm sure you've all been studying diligently."

"Ugh," Amelia groaned, shoving her books into her bag.

"Up all night swiping again?" Melody asked as she followed her friend out the double doors.

"Huh? What gave it away?"

"Come on, Lia, you only ever drool when you're thinking about guys. Who is it this time?"

"Lucas Liard. I even super liked him, too. And still, not of hint of interest in return. Blonde, 6'2, abs like a god, dazzling blue eyes, a smile that literally drenches me... *and* he likes foie gras! Do you know how difficult it is to fine someone, not just a guy, who likes foie gras? I mean, it's like we're a match made in Heaven, like God sat on his little throne up in the sky and stitched us together!" Amelia exclaimed and threw her hands up in the air, her bag dangling off her right shoulder.

"Bleh! Disgusting! I don't know how you eat that. One sniff, and I wanna gag."

"But, Mel, aren't Lucas and I just *perfect* for each other?! Just meant to be?"

"Yeah, perfect in a world of delusion. He hasn't even liked you back. Do you know anything about him beyond what his profile says?"

"Duh! He goes to Harper College, is on the lacrosse team, and has two sisters."

Melody rolled her eyes.

"What?"

"I meant, anything *other* than what you found stalking his social media."

"Well... no, not yet. But it's still early on in our relationship. There's plenty to learn about each other!"

Melody blinked and continued to stare at her friend. "You okay?"

That's when Amelia broke down and started to wail. "Why is it that all the good ones never like me back? Sixteen months! It's been exactly sixteen months and two days since David left me, and I *still* can't find another boyfriend!"

"Maybe you just need a longer break. You know, Lia, it's good to just be alone sometime." Melody adjusted the strap of her bag on her shoulder, checking her phone for the time. "Can we go get lunch now? I'm starving."

But Amelia ignored her question. "You have Kyle. He adores you so much that he'll literally kiss your feet. You don't know how difficult it is for those who are still single."

Her patience weakening, Melody raised her tone. "Well, Lia, I don't know what to tell you. Your standards are too damn high, and you try to date people who are completely out of your league! Let's face it, we're both sevens at best. Of course, you're gonna fall if you go chasing after a ten! Maybe it's time you find another seven."

"Lower my standards? Are you serious? David was a nine. It's either I go higher than that, or I'm staying single for the rest of my life."

Melody shrugged her shoulders and started walking away. "Guess you're staying single forever. I'm getting pizza."

LATER THAT NIGHT, Amelia leaned against her pillow on her bed and pulled up the app. According to her, there isn't a better feeling in the world than changing into her cozy robe, climbing under her sheets, and scrolling through her phone.

"Nerd. Nerd. Gap tooth. Ugly. Ugly. Gross. Ew. Ugly.

Short. Ugly. Ugh! Why is this so hard?!" She'd been on her phone for the past two hours, scrolling nonstop, guy after guy, and not a single match. She paused and swiped the app away, pulling up Lucas' social media profile, smiling as if his smile on one of his pictures were smiling back at her, leaning in to kiss her phone gently. "It's been almost a full day since I super liked you. Why are you ignoring me?!"

And suddenly, her phone started to ring. Her mother.

"Hey, Mom, what's up?"

"Hi, honey, how's school treating you? You doing okay? I can't wait to see my little girl's name on the Dean's List."

"Aw, come on, Mom. College is supposed to be about having fun, finding myself. You can't seriously expect me to study all the time."

"But your brother—"

"I'm not like Jason, okay? He's a nerd! His nose is always shoved inside a book that I bet he has no life!"

"Amelia!"

"Sorry, I get that you want me to go to med school like him, but that's not me, Mom. Let me make my own decisions for once." There was a loud sigh on the other line. *"What is it, Mom? Everything okay?"*

"What? Oh, yes, everything's great, dear. Listen, can you come home tomorrow night? I know you're on spring break next week, and I was thinking you could spend a few days at home, with your family. Your Aunt Evelyne's visiting Friday night before going on her business trip, and it'll be good for us to all have dinner together."

Amelia looked over at her calendar. She hated visiting home, particularly because she always got compared to Jason whenever she's around her family. But she hadn't been in over five months, and it wasn't like she had anything else planned for the next upcoming days. Honestly, she'd hoped to spend all of spring break swiping through more potential suitors.

Every day she isn't using the app means another day spent without her new boyfriend.

"Fine, I'll drive back tomorrow night."

"Wonderful! I'll even make your favorite, pot roast and garlic baked potatoes. I love you, honey."

"Love you too, Mom."

When she hung up, Amelia reached under her dorm bed and grabbed a bag of family-sized sour cream and onion chips along with a beer.

"It's going to be a long night," she whispered and pulled up the app.

Chapter Two

"Can I get an iced coffee, please? Extra-large?" Amelia asked the freckled-faced teenager at the counter of the university's coffee shop. She barely had the strength to stay awake in English Lit, and now she had to drive two and half hours back home to her parents.

"I really, really don't think you're in the condition to drive home, Lia. What if you pass out on the wheel?" Melody asked as she grabbed her own drink from the teenager, a medium matcha green latte with extra foam.

"No, I canceled on them the past three times. I can't do it again."

"Why not just go home tomorrow? I mean, you *do* have an entire week to spend with them," Melody suggested and took a sip from her cup.

But Amelia shook her head. "Can't do that, either. My Aunt Evelyne is coming over tonight before leaving town for a few days. My family already sees me as a disappointment. The least I could do is show up for dinner."

"Lia, you're a mess, you know that?"

Amelia laughed and reached over to grab her coffee. "I sure

do, but a *hot* mess." Then she paused. "Are you sure you don't wanna come spend spring break with my family? It beats sitting in your dorm all by yourself."

Melody nodded. "Yeah, it's my fault, anyway. I forgot to remind my parents about spring break before they booked their flight to Puerto Rico. But it's all good. Kyle's coming to visit for a few days. At least, I'll have him to keep me company. Besides, I should really study for that physics final if I want to make the Dean's List this semester."

"Ugh, not you, too."

"What do you mean?"

"My mom went on and on last night about the fucking Dean's List, and how I should be more like my brother, and I'm just so tired of hearing about it!" She took a sip of her coffee. "Why can't I just do what I want? Live my own life."

"You mean fawning over boys and drooling in class?" Melody teased.

A slight smile drew over Amelia's face. "Oh, shut up!" And she laughed.

"So, how'd your search go last night? Did Lucas get back to you?" Melody changed the subject as they walked over to a vacant table. The coffee shop was much emptier than usual, as most of the students had already left for their break.

Amelia pulled out her phone to check if there were any new messages. Nothing. "I think he's playing hard to get."

"I think he's playing not interested." Melody burst into laughter and tilted her head back.

"That's not funny! I truly believe that Lucas Liard is the man for me. He just hasn't realized it yet. He'll come around soon, trust me."

"If you say so."

AN HOUR LATER, Amelia said farewell to her friend and walked toward the parking garage with her suitcase. She knew she didn't need much, as her room back home still had most of her things, but she didn't want to be caught in a situation where she didn't have her loyal stilettos or her sexy black dress with her.

She stepped into her car and scouted the area near her school for somewhere that was still open. The three cups of caffeine today weren't nearly enough to balance out her two hours of sleep.

"Closed. Closed. Closed," she read sign after sign out loud as she rounded each corner. "The perk of living in the middle of nowhere truly is that everything closes before seven."

A few minutes later, she spotted a gas station. Not the cleanest, but it'll do for a quick stop. She quickly pulled into a spot and walked inside, heading back toward the refrigerated section of the store. When she reached in to pull out a can of energy drink, she heard a deep voice call out her name.

"Amelia? Amelia, is that you?"

Amelia spun around and found herself staring at a lanky man around her age whom she'd never seen before. He had rounded red glasses over his eyes, messy light brown hair, and wore a long sleeve tee that looked way too oversized for him.

"Uhm, yeah... Do I know you?" she asked, backing away slightly in hopes that he'd get the hint.

"No, but you should. I'm Patrick. I super liked you on Hooked three days ago, and I never heard back from you."

Hooked, Amelia thought. *That's my app.* "Oh... uhm... yeah... sorry, I've... been super busy lately. Haven't been on the app much." *Ugh, I wanted Lucas, and instead, this freak shows up?*

"Bummer, that sucks. Well, we're both here now! What do you say we go out and grab a drink? And then maybe back to my place for some R&R?"

A small stream of bile rose in her throat, and she quickly forced herself to push it back down. "I can't, sorry. I'm actually on my way home for spring break. I'm sure you know how parents can be when you're late." *I never thought I'd be so grateful to go home.*

"Well, do you wanna swap numbers at least? That way, we can chat during break, and then hang out when you get back? There's this new arcade near here that I've been dying to go to. What do you say we make it our first date?"

Amelia felt her heart bleeding inside her chest. *Why won't this kid just go away? There's a reason I never responded to him. I don't like him. I don't like you!* But she couldn't say that to him, especially not to his face. Confrontation had always been her Achilles' heel, and she just wanted to get the hell out of there as soon as possible.

"I... I have to go. I'll message you back. But I really have to run," she stammered.

"Just quickly swap numbers. What if I don't see you again?" He began following her.

Then that surely wouldn't be the worst thing in the world. "I'll message you," she stammered again.

She spun around on her heel and quickly made her way toward the front door.

"Hey, what about your drink?" Patrick called out after her.

I'd rather risk my chance passing out at the wheel than stay another minute around this loser. "Don't need it anymore. Thanks!" And she pushed her way out the door, sprinting to her car and driving away before he had a chance to catch up to her. Her heart was beating fast, definitely not tired anymore, and she fumbled with her phone to dial Melody's number, putting her on speaker while she continued to drive.

"Lia? Aren't you heading down to your parents?"

"I was—am. Driving as we speak. You won't *believe* what just happened to me."

"Hold on, Lia. Kyle's on hold on the other line. I'll let him know I'll call him back."

Melody had been Amelia's friend ever since Freshman orientation. They met while they were on the same team together during a team-building exercise, and they instantly bonded, becoming the best of friends and sharing all their secrets with each other. So much so that Melody would immediately know when Amelia was about to enter one of her long rants.

"Alright, I'm back." Amelia heard on the other line. "What's up?"

"I was just at a gas station, trying to get an energy drink, when some loser walked up to me and asked me out, pressured me to give him my number. He said he super liked me on Hooked and, for some reason, the freak assumed that we *have* to go out. I had to fucking run out of there like my life depended on it! Didn't even get my drink. Can you believe the audacity of that guy? Coming up to me like that and demanding a date?"

"Well...," Melody began. "Was he at least cute?"

"If he was, do you really think I'll be on the phone with you right now? Calling him a loser?" Amelia could almost hear her friend shrug. She knew her all too well. "What?" she asked.

"Remind you of anyone?" Melody asked, her voice sounding smug.

"No, should it?"

"Two words, Lia. Lucas Liard."

Amelia shook her head. "No, no! This is nothing like my situation with Lucas. *I'm* not a four-eyed freak with a shirt that's too big for me. It's completely different! I'm not a loser!"

"Then why hasn't Lucas messaged you back? What if *you* were to approach *him* suddenly out in public? You don't think he'd run away, just like you did?"

"No! Maybe... possibly. Shit, I *am* a four-eyed freak with a shirt that's too big for me, aren't I?" Amelia asked, her voice cracking at the realization.

"Sounds like it to me."

Amelia fell silent, tears welling in her eyes. How could she have been so foolish, obsessing over some stranger who didn't even care about her enough to say hi?

"You okay, Lia?" Melody asked when she realized no one was answering her.

Amelia sniffled. "Yeah, yeah, I'm fine."

"Hey, don't worry about any of that, okay? Take a few days off from the dating life. Spend some quality time with your family. I'm sure they'll appreciate it."

Probably the sanest thing Amelia had heard all day. "You have a point. Thanks, Mel."

"Drive safe!"

NEARLY THREE HOURS LATER, Amelia pulled into the driveway of her childhood home. She could see her Aunt Evelyne's bright purple jeep from a block away. Her aunt was never one to keep things subtle. She was always the loudest, flashiest, and always wanted to be the center of attention, the complete opposite of her younger sister, Amelia's mother. She loved her aunt, as much as she loved the rest of her family, but there's just something about being around her for an extended period of time that made her want to rip out all her hair, strand by strand.

Amelia reached into her pocket to fish out her keys when she reached the front door. She couldn't remember the last time she even used them, surprised that her dad hadn't changed the lock. Bracing herself for endless hugs and kisses when she walked in, she, instead, found herself face-to-face with a tall, brunette man with radiant green eyes and broad shoulders.

"Hello, you must be Amelia. My name's Alistair. Alistair Haynes," he greeted her with a dazzling smile and sparkling white teeth.

"Hi...? Uhm, I'm sorry, but am I in the right house? I could've sworn—"

"Amelia, darling! There you are!" Aunt Evelyne suddenly danced out of the kitchen wearing a floral print apron that nearly blinded her eyes. "So nice to see your beautiful face again!"

"Hey, Aunt Evelyne," Amelia murmured, slightly heaving, when she aggressively pulled her into a hug.

"I see you met Alistair. He'll be joining us tonight for dinner." Amelia looked up at her aunt and saw her grinning from ear to ear, shifting her head back and forth between this man and Amelia herself.

"Am I missing something here? Who is he?" Amelia demanded from her aunt. Then she turned back to Alistair. "Sorry to be rude," then she turned back to her aunt, "but am I supposed to know him?"

Aunt Evelyne smiled. "You will soon enough, dear. You will soon enough."

As ominous as that sounded, Amelia barely had time to register what she'd meant before her mom popped her head out from the kitchen and announced, "Dinner's ready!"

"After you." Alistair gestured to Amelia and followed behind.

Quite the gentleman. I wonder what circus he came from.

Amelia's father carved out a heaping portion of pot roast for everyone when they arrived into the dining room, with only two seats left for Alistair and Amelia... right next to each other. *Something smells fishy*, Amelia thought. *And it's not just Aunt Evelyne's pits.*

Dinner was quiet at the start, with her mother starting mundane conversations about the same three topics she always conversed about: work, Jason, and how Amelia should strive to be more like Jason. By this point, she'd learned to just tune her out, focus on the potatoes in front of her while she babbled on and on.

"Amelia? Amelia!"

Amelia popped her eyes wide at the voice yelling at her. It was her mother, standing at her spot with her hands on her hips.

"What is it?" Amelia asked.

"Your Aunt Evelyne has a special announcement." She looked over to where Aunt Evelyne was seated, as did everyone else.

"Amelia, darling, you must be dying to know why this handsome young man here has decided to grace us with his presence and join us for dinner tonight," she began.

"I guess?"

"Well, truth is, I have found you a potential new husband, Alistair Haynes."

"What?!" Amelia jumped up from her seat, pushing her chair back far behind her. She shook her head, refusing to believe what she had just heard. *A husband?* "Are you insane?! I'm only twenty-one! I haven't even graduated yet. I still have my whole fucking life ahead of me, and you're already selling me off to some dude I've only just met?"

"Amelia!" Her mother hissed. "Be respectful!"

"I'm sorry if I'm intruding," Alistair began to say to Amelia, "but I was under the impression that you'd already been informed of this situation."

She crossed her arms. "Well, I haven't. Someone care to explain it to me?"

Aunt Evelyne cleared her throat loudly and began to explain. "You see, my darling Amelia. For years, I've seen you go from boy to boy, being used by people who don't deserve you. It pains me greatly to see you wear your heart on your sleeve, just to have it broken over and over again. You deserve someone better, my dear. You deserve a man." She gestured her head toward the man beside Amelia. "Alistair here, is the son of a friend of mine, Merlyn. I met him just last week when Merlyn invited me over for some tea and biscuits, and to catch up on each other's lives. But enough about me. Alistair is a wonderful young man, smart, kind-hearted, and one day, will become a very respectable doctor. He's in medical school, you know?"

Amelia simply rolled her eyes. Just the thought of being around another doctor, who'll do nothing but show her up, was enough to make her lose interest already.

"And what if I say no?" Amelia bluntly asked.

"Amelia! Can I speak to you alone in the kitchen, please?" her mother suddenly interjected.

Probably to yell at me again, Amelia thought. Nevertheless, she pushed back her chair and followed her mother into the next room, the lingering smell of pot roast making its way into her nostrils and making her stomach growl.

"What is it?" she asked.

"I need you to stop being so rude to your Aunt Evelyne."

"Why? She's trying to pawn me off to some guy I don't even know, and *I'm* the one who needs to be respectful?"

"Yes." Her mother nodded.

"No! I refuse! It's my life, not hers!"

"Amelia, please, listen to me. I didn't want to have to tell you this, not yet anyway, but your Aunt Evelyne is very, very sick. She's only sixty-two, but she's been diagnosed with stage four Leukemia, and she doesn't have much time left. Her only wish is to see that you don't live the rest of your life unhappy. She loves you; she only wants what's best for you."

"Dying? Aunt Evelyne?" Amelia's jaw dropped open in shock. She couldn't believe what she was hearing. What was supposed to be a relatively decent family dinner turned into something much darker, and she was stuck in the middle of it.

"Yes, honey. So, please, even if you decide that you don't want to marry Alistair, just go out with him, for your aunt's sake."

"Just one date?" Amelia asked, her tone much quieter, her lips trembling.

"Three. Your Aunt Evelyne is a very superstitious woman, and she believes that it'll take at least three dates with Alistair before you're able to decide whether you like him or not."

"Just three? You sure?"

"Positive. Just three dates, and if you decide you never want to see him again, then we won't fight you on it, and you can go back to living life as you want. But, please, honey, humor your Aunt Evelyne. She worked so hard to arrange this."

Amelia huffed. She still hated the idea of being set up, but three dates were hardly a chore for her dying aunt. Besides, how bad could it be? She peeked out into the dining room and saw Alistair smiling back at her, waving. And it certainly didn't hurt that he was a gift to the eyes.

After calming herself down and pushing back in her tears, Amelia smoothed down her frayed hair and made her way back in to join the rest of her family. Without looking at anyone else, she walked straight up to her Aunt Evelyne and said, "Okay, Aunt Evelyne. I will go out with Alistair."

Chapter Three

"OMG, Lia. I can't believe you're going out on an arranged date!" Melody screamed over the phone as Amelia sat in front of vanity to put on her lipstick. "This is so unlike you!"

"Ugh, don't remind me. And it's not like I really have a choice. I have to do this for my Aunt Evelyne. It's the least I could do."

"Yeah, sorry about your aunt, man. That's rough. I don't know what I'd do if I were in your shoes."

Amelia chuckled. "Sit in front of a mirror and plaster lipstick all over yourself like a doll?"

Melody joined in. "Yeah, probably. So, tell me about this guy. He cute?"

"Eh, he's not Lucas Liard, but he's not the worst looking guy in the world. Green eyes, dark hair, broad shoulders—" Amelia began.

"Oh, sounds sexy!" Melody interrupted.

"Really, Mel?"

"What? You know I'm a sucker for green eyes. Why else do you think I'm with Kyle?" Melody exclaimed.

"Uhm... because he treats you like a queen?"

"Nah, definitely the green eyes," Melody teased.

"Amelia, honey! Alistair's here!" Amelia heard her mother call up from downstairs.

"Shit, Mel, I gotta go. He's here, and I'm still in my bra." Amelia leaned in closer to her phone, ready to hang up.

"Just go like that. I'm sure he'll love it even more."

"Oh, shut up." Amelia laughed. "Alright, I gotta go."

"Call me after! I wanna know how it went."

Amelia quickly agreed and hung up. She then finished putting on the rest of her face and rushed into her closet. She looked through the racks, nothing but old T-shirts and ripped jeans. It wasn't like she'd been very keen on impressing the guy, but she couldn't show up looking like she'd just roughed it up with the boys when he was probably decked out in a suit. She could at least *make* an effort to look halfway decent.

"Amelia!" her mother called up again, her voice beginning to grow impatient.

"I'm coming!" she shouted back. "I *could* wear the black dress I brought home, but that might give him the wrong idea."

She rummaged quicker through her racks of clothes and eventually found a floral skirt that extended down to her knees, and threw on a white blouse that she hadn't worn since her cousin's wedding. After shoving her feet into a pair of heels that tore at her ankles, she walked over to look at herself in the mirror.

"Well, I hope Alistair likes going out with grannies," she mumbled.

When she made her way downstairs, Alistair was sitting on the couch with her Aunt Evelyne, sipping on some tea and enjoying her mother's famous coffee cake.

"Don't fill yourself up too much," Amelia joked, and he looked up at her.

"Wow, Amelia." Alistair smiled and stood up to greet her with a light hug. "You look amazing."

"Seriously?" She stepped back and raised a brow. "You sure I don't look like I belong in a nursing home?"

He burst out in laughter. "Not at all. I think you look stunning."

"Aw, darling! Look at you! Beautiful as the day you were born!" Aunt Evelyne stood up from where she was sitting and stumbled over to hug her niece.

"No, no, Aunt Evelyne. You stay there," Amelia called back. She rushed over to her aunt and slowly sat her back down onto the couch. "You're in no condition to be walking around unnecessarily like this."

"Oh, don't mind me," her aunt replied. "I'm just so happy that my little Amelia is finally going on a date with a decent man. Besides, I should be heading out soon for my trip."

"And they better get going if they don't want to be late." Amelia's father stepped into the living room to cut himself a slice of coffee cake. He took a bite and closed his eyes. "Mm, your mother truly makes the best."

Alistair took Amelia's hand and smiled down at her, his pearly whites shining beneath the warm living room light. "Shall we?" he asked.

"Wait! Before you go," her mother called out, running into the living room, "let me just grab a picture of you two. Something to remember this night by."

"Come on, Mom—" Amelia began.

"I'm sure the restaurant won't mind if we're a few minutes late," Alistair assured her.

Seven pictures later, Amelia finally found herself walking to Alistair's car, a sleek black Porsche, definitely a gem in the eyes of her parents.

"Sorry about all that, by the way," Amelia apologized. "My family can be a bit... much."

Alistair laughed. "No worries. I get it. Mine are pretty much the same. The difference is, you haven't met them yet."

"So, where are we going, anyway?"

"Your aunt made us a reservation at this swanky French restaurant in town. Honestly, I didn't even know it existed until she gave me the address. But it's right by the school on Main. I must've passed it hundreds of times before and just never noticed."

"Let me guess, it's looks like a hole in the wall on the outside, but once you walk in, you magically get transformed into a new world of luxury and royalty?" Amelia asked snidely.

"Something like that." He pulled out his phone. "Here, look. If I zoom in, see that tiny white building?" He was leaning in so close that Amelia could smell the scent of cologne on him. Old spice with a hint of vanilla. He smelled so good that she didn't want to pull away, even when he closed his phone and started the ignition.

A thirty-minute drive later, Alistair pulled into a cramped parking lot behind the same tiny white building she'd seen on his phone. It wasn't much, barely enough to fit three cars, but he managed to make it work.

"Ready?" he asked, and Amelia nodded, reaching her hand out to open the door. "Whoa, whoa, whoa. Stay there." He quickly got out from the driver's seat and jogged over to the passenger side, where he gracefully opened the door and bowed as he said, "A gentleman *always* opens the door for his lady."

Amelia smiled, unsure of whether it's a smile of adoration or cringe. Even so, it was the nicest thing anyone had done for her in a long time. The most gentleman-like thing David had ever done for her was not call her fat when she'd asked.

Just like in the picture, Maison Blanc looked like nothing more than a run-down block on the outside.

"Are you sure we're at the right place?" Amelia asked Alistair, who looked down at her with a smile and grabbed her hand.

"Positive," he said.

His warm touch made her heart skip a beat and her body shiver. She didn't know what she was feeling. Alistair was the complete opposite of the type of men she'd normally fall for. She liked bad boys, like Lucas and David. Alistair's demeanor, his kind and gentle personality, odd for Amelia to start fawning over. But she didn't pull her hand away. She couldn't. She had to at least try and enjoy the date, for her Aunt Evelyne's sake, anyway.

And when they walked inside, she felt like she'd been transformed into an entirely new world. Shiny chandeliers strung along the ceiling. Velvet curtains lined the walls and windows. And every waiter and waitress inside the restaurant were dressed in black tie attire, looking even better than Alistair and herself.

"Wow, this is fancy," Amelia whispered.

"Yeah, really is. Your aunt really knows how to go all out," Alistair whispered back.

"Good evening, sir, madam," the maître d' walked up to them and greeted. "Dinner for two tonight?"

Alistair nodded, grasping onto her hand a little harder. "Correct. Reservation under Ainsworth?"

The maître d' paused to flip through the thick book that laid in front of him. Seconds later, his head popped back up, and he said, "Ah, here it is. You're here for the lover's special!"

"Lover's special?" Amelia asked. "What's that?"

"Ah, madam, the lover's special is a very special course, the very best that Maison Blanc has to offer. Twelve courses, plus the finest of wines and the most decadent of desserts."

"Sounds fantastic," Alistair exclaimed. "I—we can't wait."

"Wonderful! Right this way."

The maître d' led the two of them through the small

crowded restaurant to a candlelit booth near the back. Amelia slid in first while Alistair slid in behind her, leaving a small gap between the two of them to avoid making it uncomfortable for her.

"Wow, this menu is exotic." Alistair read through the list of courses that they'd be served aloud. "Foie gras, escargots de Bourgogne, tete de veau. I can't even pronounce these, let alone eat them."

But Amelia was too distracted by something else, and Alistair noticed. "What's wrong?" he asked. "Looks like something's bothering you."

"I still can't get over why Aunt Evelyne booked the lover's special for us. I mean, it's only our first date, and she's already acting like we're married."

He shrugged. "I'm sure she means no harm. She just wanted us to have a nice night out, that's all. But if you don't like it, we can always go somewhere else. Burgers, maybe?"

"No, it's fine. We can stay. I just don't want to feel like we're moving too fast."

"Hey, Amelia." He turned his body slightly and held onto her hands. The tingling sensation shivered up her body once more. "We can move as slow as you like. This... experience, or whatever you wanna call it—"

"Fucked-up situation?"

"That." He smiled at her again, a look of comfort and compassion shining through his eyes as he did so. "This fucked-up situation is all new to me, too. I'm just as nervous as you are."

"So, why'd you agree to her idea, anyway?"

He sighed. Then he paused and took a deep breath. "Amber."

"Amber?"

"Yeah, Amber. She was my girlfriend. My girlfriend of

seven years, to be exact. Until... until she got killed by a drunk driver one night." He took another deep breath.

"I'm so sorry."

"Don't be. It was my fault, anyway."

"How?"

"Well, Amber was drinking at a party with some of her friends and called me to come get her, but I couldn't because I was stuck at work. Long story short, she decided to get into her car anyway and, apparently, when two drunk drivers collide, it only ends in a fatality. I told her to just stay at her friend's, but she started throwing a fit and insisted that if I didn't come get her, she'd just drive herself."

"I'm sorry," Amelia said again, feeling awkward in the moment. "Are you okay?"

Alistair sniffled. "Yeah, I'm okay. And I'm sorry for unloading all this on you. Your aunt heard about my story from my mother and was only trying to pull me out of my slump and get me back out there. Mentioned that she has a niece also going through a rough time, and that we could either be happy together or sit in that slump together. Her words, not mine."

Amelia chuckled. "Definitely sounds like her."

"So, what about your situation? What's your story?"

But she just shook her head. "I don't really want to talk about it."

"I understand." He scooted himself closer to her. "If you ever do, I'm here." And then he wrapped his arm around Amelia's shoulders.

She didn't fight it, and instead, leaned her head down against him. In that moment, it just felt right, and though she didn't want to admit it, Amelia felt herself drawn closer and closer to the stranger beside her.

Chapter Four

"Amelia, honey! Don't forget. Alistair will be here in twenty minutes to pick you up!" her mother shouted up from the base of the stairs.

Amelia rolled over in her bed, the sheets tangling in between her legs as she dragged them with her. She could feel her head pounding from the lack of sleep. Despite being miles and miles away from her dorm, she still found it difficult to force herself to put down the phone.

Lucas Liard still hadn't responded to her, not even a hint that he'd reached out. And even though she quite enjoyed her first date with Alistair, she found herself continuing to scroll through guy after guy, trying to find that *perfect* person.

It also didn't help that Melody talked her ear off last night, asking about Alistair and everything about him, from his looks to his personality, even his estimated weight.

She finally managed to roll herself off the bed and grab her phone, checking the time. Noon.

"Ugh, did I really just blow my entire morning in bed?" Amelia asked herself and grabbed a towel off from the floor. Today was her second date with Alistair, and after smelling his delicious cologne from the night before, she couldn't repay him with her stench of onions and mildew.

Amelia still didn't know how she felt about him. Alistair. Sure, he was definitely the looker, a man whom everyone would stop whatever they were doing for and gawk at his beautiful eyes and charming smile. But she still couldn't imagine herself being with him. She wanted Lucas, who was a ten. David was a solid nine, and Alistair, half past nine at best. He definitely didn't reach up to Lucas' caliber, and Amelia questioned whether she was making the right decision.

"It's three dates," she reminded herself. "Just three dates. If by the end of date three, I find that I still don't like him, I'll never have to see him again. Easy."

Ten minutes later, she hopped out of the shower and into her closet. Today was beach day, an activity that Amelia felt even more nervous about than the lover's special. She'd always been body conscious, and wearing a bikini or anything revealing was one of the worst feelings in the world for her. She didn't even know if she owned a swimsuit as she always preferred mountains over beaches.

But she couldn't blame Alistair. It wasn't like he had a say either in what their dates were going to be. Hell, he probably hated the ideas as much as she did, but he's just too polite to say anything.

Amelia spent the next few minutes rummaging through her closet again, but came up short on finding a swimsuit. She eventually settled for a mini skirt with a tank top, the closest thing she could find. She then walked back over to her vanity and ran a brush through her thick hair when she heard the doorbell ring.

"Amelia!" her mother called again.

"I'm coming!" She looked down at her brush, clumps of hair knotted everywhere. But that wasn't what she was focused on. She was focused on the engraving. *A&D*. Amelia and

David. David had gotten that brush for her on their first-year anniversary. He told her how she had the most beautiful hair he'd ever seen and wanted her to take care of it. And even though she'd thrown away most of the gifts that David had ever gotten for her, she couldn't find it in herself to throw away this brush. It had become her favorite over the years, and part of her still wanted to hold onto that memory of her first serious boyfriend.

ALISTAIR WAS GLOWING beneath the sun rays when Amelia made her way downstairs. He had a towel slung over his left arm, his hair slicked back, and his tanned abs glistening as he leaned against the doorway. He had on swimming trunks and carried a picnic basket, leaving little to the imagination.

"Is that what you're wearing to the beach?" he asked Amelia while raising a brow when he saw her walk down the stairs. A slight curve formed on his lips, and it looked like he was trying to hold in a laugh.

"Hey, don't judge. It's all I have. I don't go to the beach very often."

"I can tell, but you still look great."

"Aw, look at you two teasing each other! So sweet!" Amelia's mother interrupted them with a tray of warm chocolate chip cookies in her hands. "I remember when your father and I used to tease each other. Of course, now he barely remembers my name. Here, take a few of these cookies before you go. I just baked them." She held the tray out in between them, nudging at them both and refusing to leave until they each grabbed one.

"Thank you, Mrs. Ainsworth," Alistair mumbled, holding the cookie up. "These smell delicious."

"Yeah, Mom, delicious. We should really get going."

Amelia jumped in as an attempt to save them both from bagging a pouch of cookies and bringing it with them.

The Jersey shore wasn't far from where Amelia's parents lived. It didn't have the best beaches, or the cleanest, and the weather wasn't the warmest on a windy March afternoon, but it was another one of Aunt Evelyne's wishes, and they didn't want to disappoint. Besides, Alistair was starting to grow hotter and hotter in Amelia's eyes every time she saw him. And those abs, those sexy abs that she just wanted to run her fingers over... they were enough to make her second guess her choice in men.

When Alistair pulled up into the parking lot of Cape May, they realized that theirs was the only car there.

"There's nobody here," Amelia mumbled.

"I kinda figured. It's pretty chilly out today. Why your aunt decided to choose the coldest day of the week for an activity meant for the heat is beyond me." He turned to Amelia. "We can go if you like. Somewhere indoors and warm."

But Amelia shook her head. "No, let's stay. I've never been to the beach when there's nobody else here. This might actually be fun."

"I agree! No drunk dads chasing after their screaming kids. No beach ball bouncing off my head when I'm trying to enjoy the sun."

"Man, sounds like a rough experience. I never thought I'd meet someone who hates the beach more than I do." Amelia smiled and took a bite of her cookie.

Alistair smiled back and wiped away a crumb from the corner of her mouth. "I don't hate it per se, more like I hate people ruining the experience for me."

"I know the feeling."

"But, hey, enough talk about how much we both hate people. We have the entire beach to ourselves. Let's go out there and enjoy it!" Alistair reached into the back and grabbed the towel and basket. Then he skipped over to Amelia's side and opened the passenger door for her. "Shall we?" he asked, extending a hand out to her.

"We shall," she responded and grabbed it, allowing him to lift her off her seat, her skirt bunched up behind her.

He continued to hold her hand as he led her out to the vast open shore before them. The waves swayed gently across the water, colliding with the sand before stealing some away as they retreated to where they started. Alistair unfolded the towel just a few feet from the frigid water, and they both sat down and leaned back, their elbows digging into the sand and creating craters beneath them.

"Tell me, Amelia. Why don't you like going to the beach?" Alistair asked after staring out into the ocean for quite some time.

"When did I say I don't like it?"

"You didn't. But you did mention how you don't go often, and your lack of a swimsuit makes me think that you prefer going somewhere else during your free time."

"It's true. I'm more of a mountain girl. There's just something about standing up at the tallest peak you can find and looking down at the vast wonders below you that can't be replaced by water and sand, you know?"

"I totally get what you mean. I myself enjoy mountains much more than beaches also. But I think the journey is what I'm more drawn to than the destination. It just feels very rewarding knowing that despite the struggle, the hard work I put into something will eventually pay off." Alistair agreed.

"So, would you say competition is more your style than remaining laidback and passive?" Amelia asked, causing Alistair to form a perplexed look on his face.

"Uhm, I guess. I tend to see myself as a go-getter."

"Well...," Amelia quickly stood up and tapped Alistair on

the shoulder, "you're it! Catch me before I reach the lifeguard post, and you win." She bolted off, her laughter trailing behind.

"Oh, you're on," Alistair shouted back and quickly stood up, running after her.

Amelia was a track star in high school, and was pretty fast for a girl. She saw herself as a competitive person as well, and she was certain that she'd win the race. However, less than ten feet from the finish line, Amelia found herself being hoisted into the air. Alistair had caught up to her and grabbed her by the waist, swinging her in the air, the two of them laughing.

"Gotcha!" He chuckled. Then he swung Amelia around one more time before laying her down against the stand, hovering over her as he said, "Told you I'm competitive. I also had an unfair advantage. I was a track star in high school."

"So was I!" Amelia yelled back. "I just don't have ten pounds of muscle in each leg to propel me forward." She playfully hit Alistair on the chest, her fingers trailing down his abs as she brought her hand back into herself.

The two fell silent for a moment as they both gazed into each other's eyes.

"Are you feeling what I'm feeling?" Alistair finally asked.

"Cold?" Amelia responded.

"Exactly. We should get back to the car. We can eat our lunch in there."

Amelia nodded, and as she stood up, Alistair wrapped his strong arms around her. She could feel his hard abs pressed against the side of her body, and she felt her heart skipping faster and faster as he breathed down her neck. He'd pulled her so close to him that any closer, they'd become one person. And when Alistair thought she wouldn't notice, he leaned down and kissed the top of her head, causing a smile to form on Amelia's face.

When they eventually got back to the car, Alistair cranked

the heat up and pulled his jacket out from the trunk for her to wrap around herself. It smelled of old spice and vanilla, just like he'd smelled on their first date. She pulled it tighter around herself, crossing one leg over the other for extra warmth.

He noticed and reached his hand back to pull the towel up front. "Here, use this to warm up your legs."

"What about you? Aren't you cold?"

Alistair shrugged. "Don't worry about me. I can stand it. You need it more than I do."

"Thank you." She took a bite of the turkey and Swiss cheese sandwich that Aunt Evelyne had prepared for them, and then swallowed hard. "Hey, Alistair?"

"Yeah?" he asked after taking a bite from his own sandwich.

"I think I'm ready to talk about my past relationship now."

At that, he lowered his sandwich back down, shifted his body closer to her, and gave her his full attention. "I'm all ears. Treat me like I'm a therapist."

She giggled. "Should I lie back also?"

"If you want."

"His name's David. We met when I was finishing up high school, and he was my first serious boyfriend. He meant everything to me. But of course, I was naïve and stupid enough to believe that high school sweethearts really were that common. He didn't always treat me the best, using me and treating me like I was his slave, but I let it go. I thought that's how relationships are supposed to be." She paused for a minute, and Alistair reached a hand out to tuck a strand of hair behind Amelia's right ear. "But I was foolish," she then continued, "to believe that he actually loved me the way I loved him. Two months before we finally broke up, I found a pair of panties in the back seat of his car."

Alistair continued listening without saying a word while he reached over to hold her hands in his.

"Can you believe it? I caught him cheating on me, and I still stayed, telling myself that it's just a mistake, and that he still loves me. He didn't even deny it!" She sighed. "Anyway, two months after that, he found out that he'd knocked her up, got her pregnant, and just dumped me without saying another word. Since then, I've stopped going out on dates until I know I've found the perfect one. I can't risk getting hurt again."

"Do you think it's a mistake that you're here with me now? Do you think I'll hurt you like David had?" Alistair squeezed tighter.

"Honestly," Amelia admitted, "I thought so at first. I thought my aunt was tired of me being single, so she forced me to go out with you. Now? Now I'm not so sure."

"What do you mean?"

"I like being around you, Alistair. These past two days have been amazing. I'm... I'm just not sure if you're the perfect guy yet. Please don't be mad."

And he wasn't. "It's okay, Amelia. After going through such heartbreak like you have, I completely understand why you have your standards. And I know that reaching those standards is a hard role to play. There's a chance that we're not perfect for each other. But there's also a chance that we are. You never know until you've tested out the waters."

"Thanks for understanding, Alistair. And I don't mean to offend you."

"Not offended at all." Suddenly, he leaned over closer to her, caressing her face with his hand, and planting a soft kiss on her lips. She kissed back at first, for a minute or two, before pulling away.

"I... I can't," she whispered, causing Alistair to retreat to his side of the car.

"Sorry, I'm sorry. I should've asked."

"No, no, don't be sorry. I... I just don't know how I feel about you yet." Amelia explained. "I liked the kiss. I really did. I just don't want to get my heart broken again."

Alistair remained silent, his heart obviously stunned.

"I think maybe you should take me home," she muttered with a heavy heart.

AMELIA COULDN'T SHAKE the feeling of guilt away later that night. She felt awful about the way she treated Alistair. He'd been so nice to her, and she couldn't even give him a simple kiss in return. She tossed and turned in her bed, frustrated that she couldn't shake away the feeling. Eventually, she gave up and sat up in bed. She reached over to grab her phone and dialed.

"Hello?"

"Hey, Alistair."

"Amelia? What's wrong? Is everything okay?"

"Yeah, I'm sorry for calling so late. I felt really bad about earlier, for pushing you away, and I wanted to apologize. I hope you're not mad at me."

"I'm not. Don't worry about it. It was a shock at first. I thought we were getting along, connecting. It just took me by surprise when you pushed me away."

"I know. I'm really sorry. I hope this doesn't ruin our date tomorrow."

"Nah, I'm over it. Pick you up at five tomorrow?"

"I'll be waiting."

Chapter Five

The next day, Amelia had a few hours to spare before her third and final date with Alistair. She still hadn't decided whether she wanted to continue seeing him after, or if she'd just return to her old ways on her trusty app, but that was a decision for later that night.

She scheduled an appointment at the salon to get her hair done, not to impress him, but because her hair was matted from not being groomed in over three years.

But on her way there, she saw the backside of a familiar figure, someone she knew, someone—

"David?"

The man spun around, and it was none other than her ex. "Amelia!" he greeted. "It's been awhile." He walked over to give her a hug, but her body only tensed. "What are you doing here? Aren't you still in school?"

"It's spring break. I came home to visit my family. Where's what's-her-name?"

"Rebecca? Oh, we broke it off. Funny story! Turned out the kid isn't even mine. She'd been shacking it up with guys all around town."

"You deserve it," Amelia mumbled.

"Sorry, what was that?"

"You kinda had it coming, David. Karma has its way of nipping you in the ass when you decide to screw over someone you'd promised to love forever."

David's face dropped, his usually happy-go-lucky style turning into someone who looked like they'd just been beaten twice and pushed off a cliff.

"I-I'm sorry," Amelia apologized. "I didn't mean to come off that harsh. I'm still a little bitter, you know?"

"No, you're right. I do deserve it. You shouldn't have been treated the way I treated you, and I'm truly sorry for everything I've done to you." Then he stepped closer to Amelia and held her by the hands. "Truth is, I've never stopped thinking about you, ever since we broke up—"

"You mean, ever since you dumped me," she jumped in.

"Right, I'm sorry for breaking up with you. But truth is, Amelia, I've never been able to replace you. Rebecca, she didn't mean anything to me, just a fling, something to entertain myself with, but you? Amelia, you're my everything, my high school sweetheart, and a huge part of me still believes that we're meant to be together, until the very end, just like we'd always promised each other."

"Yeah, until you cheated on me," Amelia mumbled and backed away slightly.

"Do you still love me?"

"What?" That got her attention.

"Do you still love me?" David repeated.

Amelia felt her stomach drop. Did she? To be honest, she'd spent so much time swiping from guy to guy that she never really stopped to think about David. But now that he was here, standing in front of her and professing how he felt about her, she felt all her past feelings, all the feelings she'd tried so hard to erase, all rushing back. She'd been with David for so long, her first love, and the person she created the most memories with. And she even swore to herself and Melody that she was over him, that she'd never run back to someone who could so easily run away from her.

So... so why was she finding herself being drawn back to him? Why was she suddenly remembering the happy times they've shared together?

"I... I...," Amelia stuttered.

"Say it, say it, Amelia. Do you still love me?" He held on tighter to her hands and inched in even closer. She could smell the scent of his aftershave, a scent that made her want to gag, nothing like the delicious vanilla fragrance of Alistair.

"I... I... don't," Amelia finally said and pulled her hands away. "I... I have to go."

So close. She was so close to walking straight back into her past, back into the arms of someone who left her for the wolves while he claimed another queen. And it took smelling him to help her remember that she didn't need him in her life anymore, that she was happier without him. She quickly jogged home, skipping that hair appointment she'd booked.

She had to get ready for her date with Alistair.

"AMELIA! ALISTAIR'S HERE!" Amelia heard her mother shout for the third time that night.

"I said, I'm coming!" she shouted back.

Amelia walked over to her vanity to observe her outfit for the night. She didn't know what the occasion was. The only hint she'd gotten was to "dress for a fun occasion," whatever that meant. But whatever it was, blue skinny jeans with a black leather jacket over a white T-shirt, and her hair tied up in a high ponytail, were going to have to do the trick.

"Amelia!" She heard the piercing scream of her mother once again.

"Ugh!" Amelia grabbed her purse and started to walk out the door. But then she stopped. "Forgot my gloss." And she reached into her vanity drawer to pull it out. She froze when she saw the brush. *A&D*. Still written on it as clear as day. Amelia picked it up, ran a finger across the engraving, and then threw it into her trash can before walking out the door and heading downstairs.

"Hey, beautiful," Alistair said with a smile. Amelia blushed. She hadn't heard anyone call her that in a long time, and the beautiful bouquet of roses in his hands definitely made those words sound much, much sweeter. "These are for you," he continued as if he'd read her mind, and extended his hands out to give her the roses.

"Thank you, Alistair." Amelia extended her own arms out and grabbed the roses. "I'll go put these in water straight away."

"Nope! Let me. I got it," her mother interrupted and grabbed them away. "I'll just bring these into the kitchen. You two stay here and talk."

As she skipped away, Alistair closed the gap between himself and Amelia. He reached a hand out again and tucked a strand of hair behind her ear. "Now that your mother is gone, are you going to tell me what's wrong?"

"What do you mean?"

"Amelia, I could see it on your face as soon as you walked down those stairs. Something's bothering you."

"What? No, nothing's bothering me. I'm fine!" Amelia tried her best to maintain her poker face. It wasn't like he was wrong; Alistair was definitely right. But she couldn't tell him about running into David. And how all her feelings for him shot back into her mind. It wasn't a conversation she was ready to have with someone yet, especially not with someone she'd probably stop seeing after tonight.

She looked up at Alistair while she was lost in thought, expecting to see an angry look plastered across his face, but instead, he grinned at her.

"W-Why are you smiling?" she asked.

"Heh, you're cute when you're flustered."

"I'm not flustered!"

"Hey, it's okay. You don't have to tell me anything. I was just trying to help. But like I said before, if you ever want to talk to me about anything, I'll be here. But I won't pressure you."

"So," Amelia crossed her arms in front of her chest, "where're we headed tonight?"

"Hmm, it's a surprise." Alistair continued to grin.

"Well, if I know Aunt Evelyne, I bet it's something boring and traditional like the movies or something," Amelia guessed.

"True, it would be something like that... if she had chosen for us."

"What do you mean?"

Alistair grabbed Amelia's right hand and squeezed. "Tonight's destination... is all my idea. And I want it to be a surprise."

"Well, I can't wait to see it," Amelia replied, clenching together the fingers on her other hand. She hated surprises, but she couldn't tell him that.

"Shall we get going?"

"We shall."

And as the two walked out the door, Amelia's mother followed them. "Wait! Before you go, you two have to try one of my brownies. Freshly baked, straight from the oven!"

"Mom, stop trying to make us fat." Amelia crossed her arms over her chest in protest.

"It's okay, I don't mind," Alistair responded. "I'll take one." And as he did, Amelia ushered him out the door.

"Sorry about my mother. She's not from here originally. It's traditional for her to want to fatten people up."

"Ha, yeah, I was just going to ask. Does she do this with all her guests?"

"Unfortunately, yes. So, are you ready to tell me the surprise? Where are we headed?"

"Hmm, not quite yet." When they reached his car, Alistair pulled out a blindfold. "Here, put this on."

"Why? Trying to kidnap me? I'm already willingly going out with you."

"Ah, but how else will I be sure that you'll stay with me forever?" It clearly sounded like a joke, but Amelia still got offended.

"Excuse me? What makes you think I'm yours?"

"I-I-I didn't. It was just a joke," Alistair quickly apologized. "You know, how I know you're not mine, and kidnapping you is the only way I can make you mine?" He began crazily gesturing his hands, his face growing flustered.

"Make me yours? Who do you think I am?" Amelia's face turned red. She knew she was unnecessarily taking her anger out on Alistair. Seeing David today just brought back all the bad memories of her past.

"I'm really sorry, Amelia. Truly. I didn't mean to offend you or hurt you. I just thought it was a funny joke, you know, with the blindfold." Then he shoved it back into his pocket. "But if that bothers you, you don't have to put it on. We can just go, if you'd like. Or we can cut this date short, and you can go back home. Whatever you want. I just want to make you happy."

Amelia's facial muscles loosened their tension, and her eyes of anger turned into eyes of sadness. "No, we can go. It's my fault. I get that you were only trying to make a joke, and I definitely overreacted. I'm sorry. Can you forgive me?"

Alistair was quick to smile and embrace her into a hug. "Of course! We all make mistakes, say things we shouldn't. I get it. It's no big deal!" Then he released the hug and jutted out his elbow. "Shall we?"

"We shall." Amelia looped her arm through the gap created, and he led her into the passenger side of his car. "And yes, I'll wear the blindfold."

AND IT WAS DEFINITELY to Amelia's shock when she took the blindfold off thirty minutes later, something she'd never expected to see. Alistair had pulled into the parking lot of an arcade! And Amelia hated arcades more than she hated anything else. The bright lights, the loud music, sticky kids running around, the smell of vomit and piss. And top it all off with rigged and expensive crappy games that serve no purpose other than to rob you of your entire bank account and give you a shitty teddy bear, worth no more than five bucks, in return.

"So, what do you think?" Alistair turned his head as he shut off the engine and looked at her.

Ugh, I can't tell him I hate it; that'll crush him. "I-I love it," she said instead, secretly screaming to herself on the inside.

Amelia used to love arcades as a kid, carnivals, specifically. Her parents would bring her and her brother to one once a year, and the rushed feeling of soaring high above the ground on a rollercoaster or stuffing her face with cotton candy, while her brother challenged their dad in the arcade, was one of the best she'd ever experienced.

But that all changed when she turned eleven. Their family vacation to Wildwood. The trip where she found out that she'd been forgotten. She remembered complaining of stomach pains after stuffing her face with funnel cake and ice cream, and when she came back out from using the restroom, her mother was gone. She'd promised that she was going to wait for her, that she was going to stay right outside until Amelia came back out.

And when Amelia failed to find her mother after looking around, she began to panic. She ran up and down the boardwalk, screaming for her mother, her father, her brother, anybody she recognized who could help her. But with no luck. When she decided to try the arcade, hoping that her father and brother were still battling it out, she found the place much scarier than she'd remembered. The bright lights, the loud sounds, the screaming kids and adults. They were all just too much handle for a young child who was already stressed out about being left alone.

Abandoned.

"Mom?" She remembered crying out loud, only to be pushed to the ground by a horde.

It took several hours later and a long wait at the security office for Amelia to eventually find out that Jason had injured himself while playing Dance Dance Revolution, and both her parents were in such a rush to take him to the hospital that they'd completely forgotten about her.

"It was just an accident," they'd say. But deep down, Amelia knew they wouldn't have done the same if she were the one to have gotten injured.

"Great! Ready to head inside? I can't wait to show you my favorite games." Alistair clapped his hands together in excitement, and once again, rushed to the other side to open the passenger door for her.

But when Amelia walked in, all the memories of her past came rushing back. The lights. The screaming children. The distinct stench of putrid vomit mixed with overly buttery popcorn. She held her breath, trying her best to not hurl when Alistair pulled her toward the basketball hoops.

"Challenge you in a game?" he asked, picking up a ball and handing it over to her.

Amelia shook her head and pushed it away. "No, thanks. It's not really my thing. But you go ahead. I'll watch."

Alistair scrunched his forehead and rubbed his chin dramatically with his fingers. "Are you sure? We can always go and play something else! Anything you want!"

"I'm sure." Amelia nodded her head. "I'm more of a watcher, anyway." *More of a watcher? Did I really just say that? What a stupid thing to say!*

"Alright, if you insist. Watch me make this awesome trick shot!"

Amelia watched with boredom as Alistair spun around in a circle before shooting the ball, touching nothing but net as the ball smoothly slid into the hoop.

"Yes!" he shouted.

The rest of the night continued similarly as Alistair played every game possible inside the arcade, a true kid in a candy store, as Amelia just stood by his side, yawning and playing on her phone. She made sure Alistair wasn't looking as she discretely scrolled through Lucas' social media profile, admiring the tanned abs and glistening smile in his most recent pictures.

"Hey, Amelia!" A voice distracted her, and when she looked up, Alistair was holding a pink stuffed teddy bear. "I got this for you. Took all my tickets, but I really wanted to get you something."

She grabbed it and muttered, "Thanks."

"What's wrong? Do you not like it?"

"It's okay, I guess. It's just that I could've bought this at Walmart for half the cost of what it took to play all these games."

Alistair's face fell. "Well... I thought it was a nice gesture. We had fun, and I only played all those games so I could win enough tickets to get something for you."

But Amelia shook her head. "No, Alistair. *You* had fun. *You* spent all this money getting a cheap toy. All I did was watch you."

"B-But you said that's what you wanted. I'm sorry, Amelia. I didn't realize you weren't having any fun. I asked you several times if you wanted to play, but you kept saying no."

"Because I hate arcades! I'm sorry, Alistair. Here, take your bear back. I'm going home. Thanks for the date, but I don't think there will be another one."

His face fell even harder, low enough to make Amelia feel sorry for him if she wasn't already in such a frustrated mood. "I understand. Can I at least take you home?"

"No, I'll just call my mom." Amelia quickly threw back and walked out the glass doors.

Chapter Six

A week later, back at her dorm, Amelia found herself calling her ex, David.

"*Hello?*"

"*Hey, David. It's me, Amelia.*"

"*Oh, what do you want?*"

"*I was just thinking. Remember how when we ran into each other the other day, you said that part of you still believes that we're meant to be together?*"

"*Yeah...?*"

"*Well, I was wondering... do you want to give us another shot? See if this whole high school sweetheart thing will really pay off? Maybe we were too young to commit when we dated before, but we've both grown now. It might actually work out.*"

"*Uhm, no. I don't think so.*"

"*Why not? You said we could work.*"

"*Yeah, Amelia. I did. But when I asked you if you still loved me, you flat out said no and ran away. That fucking hurt. I stood there, out in the open, vulnerable, and you just rejected me. No way in hell am I falling for your mind tricks again.*"

"*But David, that wasn't—*"

"Goodbye, Amelia."

And just like that, David hung up. And when she tried calling again, she found out that he'd blocked her. Her heart felt broken, crushed, just like it had felt when he left her the first time. After such a horrible date with Alistair last week, she was sure that David was the one for her, and that no one else could ever compare. Unfortunately for her, he didn't have the same thought, and Amelia was left all alone again.

She even tried to take her mind off the pain by resuming her daily ritual of scrolling through eligible bachelors, but even those didn't seem as interesting to her anymore. She didn't know what she was feeling, but her mind felt distracted by something. By someone.

"Ah, Ms. Ainsworth, I see that, once again, you're using my class as your own personal naptime." Amelia flung her head up and found Professor Ambone and the rest of her class staring at her, as if her life were on a never-ending loop, and spring break had never happened.

"Huh? I-I'm sorry. I-I'm sorry. It won't happen again," Amelia stuttered.

"Well, I sure hope not, especially if you pass this final exam and move on from my class."

"What? Exam?" Amelia turned to Melody as Professor Ambone proceeded to hand out the small blue notebooks.

"Aw, Amelia, don't tell me you forgot! Did you really stay up all night again swiping instead of studying?"

"What? No, I just couldn't sleep, that's all. My mind's been distracted lately."

"Lucas again?"

"Ahem!" Professor Ambone suddenly appeared in front of them. "Ladies, time to put the chit-chat away."

Amelia gulped as he placed the small blue notebook in front of her, followed by a thick stack of papers she assumed were the problems. She took one look at the first one, and her eyes opened wide in horror. She looked over at Melody, who was quickly scribbling away, and then she looked at Professor Ambone, who was staring straight at her from the front, as if he were expecting her to do something she shouldn't. She quickly looked down at the first problem again, groaning, flipping through to the other pages to see if she knew any of the other ones, and started scribbling away.

After class, she met up with Melody in the cafeteria, throwing a slice of pizza onto her tray just to have it, but Amelia found that she didn't have an appetite. When she sat down, Melody was already at their favorite spot, digging into her salad.

"You left class pretty quickly today," Melody said. "I'm guessing the exam was a breeze for you?"

"Are you kidding me?! I didn't know a single answer. I only handed my stuff in so I could get the hell out of there. I could only sit there and stare for so long. I'm pretty sure I failed."

"Lia! Why didn't you study? I reminded you every day for the past week to make sure you're prepared. What the hell were you doing instead?"

"I don't even know." Amelia slid into her seat. "It's like, ever since I came back from spring break, my mind has been elsewhere."

She nodded. "Is it because of Alistair?"

"Alistair?"

"Yeah, whatever happened to him? He seemed like such a perfect match for you," Melody asked, taking a bite of her salad.

Amelia shrugged. "Just didn't really connect like I'd hoped. Besides, I only went out with him to make Aunt

Evelyne happy. Three dates. That's what I promised. Nothing more. He's not really my type."

"You know, Amelia, for someone who says she wants a boyfriend, you sure are awfully picky. I thought Alistair was a great guy. Incredibly sexy, too."

"Yeah, but he's not... he's not Lucas Liard."

Then suddenly, her phone rang. Amelia pulled it out of her jacket pocket and saw a message from none other than Lucas Liard himself.

LUCAS

Hey, Amelia. Saw you super liked me. Down to grab a drink tonight?

"Oh my god, oh my god!" Amelia practically danced in her seat. "You'll never guess who just asked me out! Lucas! Do you know how long I've been waiting for this moment? How much I've been obsessing over him?"

"Oh, I sure do. But don't you think it's a bit odd how he blew you off for so long, and he's just *now* getting back to you? If he really liked you, he wouldn't have waited."

"Nah, I'm sure he just had other things going on. I mean, it's Lucas Liard, the most eligible bachelor in town, maybe in the entire county! And he wants to go out with *me*. Me! I can't pass up the chance."

"Hmm, I don't know, Amelia. I don't trust him. What if he's just using you?"

"Mel, look, I don't have time for your rational judgment right now. I gotta go. I need as much time as I can get to prepare for tonight. I'll call you later!" Amelia rushed through her sentence and grabbed her bag, leaving her pizza to grow cold on the cafeteria table and rushing out the door.

"Do I look stunning, or do I look stunning?" Amelia asked herself as she danced in front of the floor-length mirror in her dorm later that night. "Fit to be Lucas Liard's queen, I might add?"

The time was seven, and Lucas said he'd be here to pick her up for their date. Amelia had been preparing for the past three hours, making sure her makeup was perfect, every strand of hair on her head was perfect, her face free from blemishes or wrinkles. She was finally going out on a date with the man she couldn't stop stalking, and she wanted to make a good first impression, give him something that he's never going to forget. Make him remember her forever.

"Perfect," Amelia slipped in her last earring and tucked a strand of loose hair behind her ear, "and just in time."

She picked up her phone, expecting a text from Lucas telling her that he was outside. But she saw nothing. Ten minutes soon passed, then fifteen, then thirty. Still nothing.

"I guess he's not coming." Amelia sighed and took off her shoes. "Something probably came up. I'll text him tomorrow and see if he wants to reschedule."

And then something. Her phone dinged, and it was a message from Lucas.

> **LUCAS**
>
> Hey, sorry, my car broke down, and I couldn't come get you. Do you think you can meet me at Duggard's Bar? I live right near there.

Duggard's Bar was nearly forty minutes away from where Amelia lived, and she'd let Melody borrow her car tonight since she'd expected Lucas to pick her up. She could always hail a cab, an Uber, something cozy to take her downtown, but being so late at night, it'd be a struggle just to find one that wouldn't charge her an arm and leg.

But she couldn't say no, as inconveniencing as it was for her. If she canceled on him, she may never get another chance to go out with him, killing any hope she had of being with him.

"The bus it is, I guess." Amelia quickly messaged Lucas back, telling him that she'd be there in about an hour. Fortunately for her, he quickly messaged her back, saying that he'd still be there waiting for her.

With a smile, Amelia threw her shoes back on and grabbed the little cash she had from her desk drawer. "Three dollars in singles. Should be enough to cover the fare."

A little over an hour and a dreadful bus ride later, Amelia finally made it to Duggard's Bar. It was packed when she walked in, something she was never a fan of. She tended to stay away from scenes where she struggled just to hear herself talk. But she didn't come this far just to back out now. And so, she squeezed her way through the drunken crowd to find Lucas.

When she eventually did, he was sitting at the bar, talking to a woman.

"Hey, Lucas, who's this?" Amelia asked as she approached them, gesturing to the bartender for a glass of water.

"Amelia, babe! You made it! You had me worried sick that something had happened to you," Lucas practically screamed when he saw her, the smell of alcohol pungent on his breath. "Oh, this? This is Lucy. She was just keeping me company while I waited for you." He turned to grin at Lucy, who slapped him hard across the cheek and stormed away.

"That's... weird," Amelia said. "Is she mad about something?"

"Nah." Lucas waved a hand. "Probably just on her period or something. Hey, let me buy you a drink. What's your style? Long Island? Cranny vodka?"

"Just a beer is fine."

"Simple, I like that." He gestured to the bartender. "One beer, my good man."

"Lucas, I have to ask, why'd it take you so long to message me back? I know you saw my message."

"Message? No, no, you see, my phone is a little messed up sometimes. It sends read receipts even if I hadn't actually read them. Such an odd glitch. I should really have someone take a look at it. I just saw your message last night. Figured you're cute. So, here we are!"

"That... that *is* a strange glitch." Amelia struggled to believe him, but she didn't want to risk saying anything that'd cause him to leave.

"Hey, it's a bit loud in here, don't you think? What do you say we go somewhere much quieter?"

Best idea I've heard all night. "Count me in! Where were you thinking?"

"Back to my place? My apartment's just down the road; we could walk there."

Amelia nodded and followed Lucas out of the bar and out the back door. He was walking so fast, his body swaying from side to side as he struggled to keep his drunken self upright. Amelia struggled to keep up with him, her heels stabbing into the soles of her feet as she ran.

Fifteen minutes later, Amelia stopped running when Lucas stood in front of a run-down ten-story apartment building, waving for her to hurry up. He unlocked the front door and led her up to the third floor.

"Here we are! Welcome to my bachelor pad!" he announced as they both walked in.

The first thing that Amelia noticed was the smell, the smell of musty day-old pizza and aftershave. The second thing she noticed was how much of a slob Lucas was. There were clothes strewn all over his raggedy sofa and computer, beer bottles forming a rug over the stained carpet, and pizza boxes were scattered in every corner that Amelia could find.

"Nice... nice place you have here," Amelia mumbled, pushing aside a pile of clothes to find a spot for herself to sit on the sofa. *Geez, and I thought I was messy.*

"Sorry about all the mess. I wasn't expecting to have company tonight," Lucas apologized and sat beside her. The stench of alcohol was way more prominent now that they were out of the bar.

"It's fine."

"So, Amelia," he leaned back and threw his arm over his shoulders, "tell me, what is it that you really want?"

"What do you mean?"

"I mean, why'd you wanna go out with me? Meet me at a bar?"

Amelia felt confused. She'd never been asked that question before. A date is just a date, something people do when they like each other. *Why's he interrogating me?*

"Uhm, I think you're cute, and I wanted to get to know you better."

Lucas pretended to think for a bit before shaking his head in reply. "Nah, I think you want something more than that." He leaned in closer. "I think you wanna fuck me. And you know what? I wanna fuck you, too."

Then he pounced on her, pressing his lips against hers, and began peeling off her clothes.

"Lucas, stop. You're drunk. We shouldn't do this!" Amelia struggled to speak through Lucas' slobbering lips, his roaming hands groping all parts of her body.

"I'm not drunk, just horny. Come on, I know you want this. So hot." He moved his lips down to her neck, then to her breasts, before Amelia pushed him off her and onto the ground.

"I said, no!" she screamed and pulled her clothes back around her body.

"What the hell, bitch?" Lucas screamed back from the floor. "Why the *fuck* did you wanna go out with me if you didn't want this?"

"I-I-I just wanted to get to know you."

"Bullshit! If you're not gonna put out, I want you out!"

"But Lucas—"

"I said, out!"

Amelia picked her bag off from the sofa and ran toward the door, kicking aside a couple beer bottles in the process. Tears were streaming down her face, ruining the perfectly contoured makeup that she'd spent hours putting on. Lucas turned out to be nothing like the embodiment of perfection that Amelia had longed for. He wasn't her perfect match, not even a sad attempt at a match. How could she have been such a fool, thinking that someone like Lucas, a fuck boy, would ever want anything more from her than sex?

Walking out into the cold, Amelia stood there waiting for the bus. According to the schedule online, there was still one left that ran at this hour. Tears continued to stream down her face as she thought back to how Alistair always made sure that she was warm and comfortable in his car, always her knight in shining armor and ready to pick her up.

Alistair had always been there for her, the complete opposite of David and Lucas. He understood when she overreacted, forgiving her in an instant. He was the perfect gentleman when she told him that she wanted space, and he never walked ahead of her, always remaining by her side and holding her hand, making sure that she was happy and safe.

"Alistair," Amelia said to herself. "How could I have been so wrong about you? How could I have treated you the way I did?"

Chapter Seven

That weekend, Amelia found herself driving back home once again. She'd failed her physics exam, meaning she'd have to retake Ambone's class over the summer, but that was the least of her worries.

Her Aunt Evelyne had died; she found out the morning after her disastrous date with Lucas. The Leukemia had spread to her lungs, and she died from suffocation and lack of oxygen in her sleep. Her aunt was like a second mother to Amelia, taking care of her, cooking her favorite meals, playing with her when her mother was at work. She should've been sadder, more devastated, but the events of her own shitty love life had numbed her to everything else around her.

When she arrived home, cars were piled up outside her parents' house. The door was cracked open, and Amelia made her way inside after she'd pulled into the driveway. The entire family was here, from aunts and uncles to distant cousins, even some of Aunt Evelyne's friends and co-workers.

"Amelia, darling. I'm so glad you could make it back. I'm sorry if you had other plans this weekend." Her mother had found her and pulled her into a hug. Amelia could hear her sniffling behind her, and her heart warmed.

"Hey, Mom. Of course. I wouldn't miss this for the world. How's Dad doing?"

"He's been better. He was very close with his sister, and after losing your grandfather earlier this year, it's just a little much for him to handle at the moment. Jason's out back comforting him."

"I miss her, Mom. I miss her so much!" Amelia suddenly broke out in tears and wrapped her arms around her mother, crying into her shoulder and making her dress wet.

"It's okay, honey. It's okay. Your aunt only wanted what's best for all of us. She just wanted us to be happy. As long as you're happy, she's happy." Then she pulled away. "I have to finish getting everything ready. Are you okay on your own for a bit?"

Amelia nodded and watched as her mother walked upstairs.

When she turned around and walked back into the living room, where the crowd was, she noticed the back of a familiar figure.

"Alistair," she whispered. She walked up behind him and said, "Hey."

He turned around, and even during a time of sadness and sorrow, he still shone a glimmer of hope in his eyes. "Amelia, it's good seeing you again," he said, and he leaned in for a light hug.

"Yeah... hey, do you think we can step outside for a bit and talk? In private?"

Alistair glanced down at his watch before nodding. "Sure, we still have some time before we have to head out."

He followed suit as Amelia led him outside onto the patio. It wasn't the best location, with friends and family still circulating in and out through the front door, but Jason and her father had the backyard occupied, and Amelia would rather not have them eavesdrop on her conversation with Alistair.

"What's up?" he asked, sitting down on the wooden bench in front of the house. "Is everything okay? Are you okay?"

"Yeah... I-I'm fine. I just... I just... I just..." Amelia stuttered her words and began crying, sniffing though her nostrils and trying to keep herself from completely breaking down.

"Hey, hey, it's okay." Alistair pulled Amelia in closer to him, her head leaning against his chiseled chest. She could smell the old spice and vanilla cologne that she'd been so used to and so in love with during their time together, and it only brought back memories of how happy she'd been with him. "Whatever it is, I'm here, okay? I'm here. Just let it all out."

"I'm in love with you!" Amelia suddenly shouted. Luckily, no one else was around in that moment, and the chatter inside the home was too loud for anyone to pick up anything.

"What?"

"There, I said it! I'm in love with you, Alistair. And I'm sorry it took me this long to figure it out. And I'm especially sorry for pushing you away and running off during our last date. But I've tried not thinking about you. I've tried going back to my old life. I've even tried distractions, many of which I don't even wanna tell you. But Alistair, you've treated me like no one else ever had. You see me, and you're there for me no matter how much I fuck up." Amelia took a deep breath and wiped away her tears. "Aunt Evelyne was right, and it sucks that she's no longer here to see her wish come true. But I love you, Alistair. You really *are* the perfect match for me."

"Amelia, I—" Alistair began.

"You don't have to say anything now," she interrupted him. "I just needed to get it out there. I needed you to know before it's too late." She put a finger up to his lips, but he gently pushed it away.

"Amelia, I do like you. And for a while, I thought it was love that I felt, too. But watching you push me away, rejecting me, and then now this complete change, it's making me feel a little cautious. You remind me a lot of my ex. Beautiful, fun, but also impulsive. I fear that you don't know what you want. And I fear that one day, you're either going to just walk away or get yourself into an accident that you can't recover from."

"W-What are you saying, Alistair?" Amelia's voice trembled as she spoke, and even though she asked, she knew where the conversation was headed.

"I think you need to figure out what it is you really want before anything can happen between us. I care about you, Amelia, and I only want what's best for you. You'll never be happy in a relationship if you don't know what it is you're seeking." He leaned over and kissed her on her left cheek. "We should head back inside."

⸻

OVER THE NEXT FEW DAYS, Amelia found herself fighting with her own thoughts. She thought she wanted Alistair. In fact, she was so sure of it. But then again, she also said the same about David and Lucas. Maybe she wanted all of them. Or maybe she wanted none. But either way, she didn't know where to begin finding her answer.

She was back on campus, and only a month away from the realization that she'd be locked up in school all summer for failing while the rest of her classmates got to go on vacation. Things couldn't possibly get any worse.

"How'd it go with Alistair?" Melody asked, taking a sip of her smoothie.

The spring afternoon was cozy and warm, but even the fresh air wasn't enough to snap Amelia out of her slump.

"Not so great," she answered, tossing a bread crumb over to a pack of pigeons and watching them fight over it. "He doesn't want me."

"You're kidding! I thought he really liked you!"

"Yeah, I thought so, too. But when I told him how I felt, when I told him that I love him, he rejected me."

Melody shook her head. "Wow, I can't believe what I'm hearing. What an ass!"

"No," Amelia corrected her. "He's not the ass. I am. He only rejected me because he said I was being unfair to myself, letting myself get into a relationship without really knowing what I wanted."

"Well, is he right? Do you know what you want?"

"I want him. God, Mel, I just can't stop thinking about him, dreaming about him. How do I get him back?"

"Simple, Lia, you gotta just tell him, straight from the heart. If Alistair sounds like the man that you've made him out to be, I'm sure he'll understand." She checked her phone. "Listen, I have to get going. Kyle's coming over, and we're going out to dinner."

"Have fun," Amelia mumbled. And when Melody left, she pulled out her phone and dialed Alistair's number.

The ring tone was deafening when, even after the sixth try, there was no answer. She tried again, and again, and again, only to be met with that same god-awful, gut-wrenching tone.

"I lost him. I had him, the perfect man, right at the tips of my fingers, and I just pushed him away. And now, now I'm never getting him back. I deserve it," she whispered to herself and slowly trudged back to her dorm.

But when she arrived back at her building, she saw him, none other than Alistair himself!

"W-W-What are you doing here?" Amelia stuttered in surprise. "I-I tried calling you."

Alistair smiled, that same charming grin that had Amelia swooning the first time she saw it. "I know, and I'm sorry for not picking up. I wanted to surprise you."

"And you did! What are you doing here?" she asked again.

"To ask you to marry me."

"Wait, what? Really?"

Then he burst into laughter.

"You tease!" Amelia shouted.

"I'm sorry. I thought it'd be funny, given our history. But I *did* come here to ask you out, on a real date, not a setup."

"You drove all the way up here just to ask me out on a date?"

"I sure did, and I'd do it again any day. So, what do you say? Will you go out with me, Amelia Ainsworth?"

She didn't say anything back. Instead, she jumped up, wrapped her arms around his neck, and kissed him lovingly on the lips. His mouth tasted so good, his tongue so passionately dancing in her mouth, and she didn't want to pull away.

"Wait, but I thought you didn't want anything to do with me until I figured things out, until I figured out what I wanted," Amelia asked when she pulled away.

"I thought that's what would be best for us. I didn't want us rushing into anything until we're both completely certain. But every day without you felt like I was missing a piece of myself, and I hadn't realized how much I actually do love you until you said it back. So, the hell with my dumb idea. We both love each other, so let's just be with each other!" He bent down and kissed her again, wrapping his arms around her waist and tilting her head back. "So, where would you like to go? Anywhere you want."

Amelia thought about it for a minute, her finger tapping

against her chin. "There's this new arcade near here that I've been dying to go to. What do you say we make it our first *official* date?"

The End

Stalk the Author

Website:

https://www.kathrynreign.com/

Facebook Page:

https://www.facebook.com/authorkathrynreign

Instagram:

https://www.instagram.com/authorkathrynreign/

Goodreads:

https://www.goodreads.com/author/show/21854875.
Kathryn_Reign

BookBub:

https://www.bookbub.com/authors/kathryn-reign

Three Dates